THE
CLOCKWORK
EYEBALL

Steven Poore

Other dyslexic friendly quick read titles from BOTH publishing

The House on the Old Cliffs

Ultrasound Shadow

Anchor Point

At Midnight I Will Steal Your Soul

The Breath

Sherlock Holmes and the
Four Kings of Sweden

The Man Who Would Be King

The Clockwork Eyeball

Marrakesh – 1958

Saif closed the door softly behind him as he stepped out into the narrow, shaded derb, but he knew he was already being watched. The few small windows high up in the walls that lined this quiet and anonymous alleyway were all firmly closed, their stained glass panes thick with dirt and sand that had been blown across the city. Any one of them might hide an unfriendly pair of eyes.

He resisted the temptation to look upwards as he passed underneath them.

He had no problem with people looking, just as long as they did not see him doing anything.

Two sharp turns, ducking back against the wall to avoid a freewheeling cyclist coming the other way – the man should have sounded his bell and Saif threw a half-hearted curse over his shoulder at him – and he was back onto one of the Medina's minor through routes. The palm frond lattices that covered the street cast sun-dappled patches onto everything, winking like faulty light fittings as he walked unhurriedly past the stalls and the craftsmen. More importantly, they prevented people from using the rooftops to watch and follow his progress.

He doffed his hat and bowed at the passage of a silk-suited gentleman who trailed a collection of bawling and clamouring urchins in his wake. A British tourist, without a doubt, and one who had probably made the easy mistake of over-tipping. The man strode along the street just as Britain herself bestrode the Western world. His discomfort was ill-hidden behind the mask of Imperium that all the European folk affected. But this, Saif told him silently, was not the West, and Britain did not rule here.

Two tightly-wound and soft-clicking mechs – imports, plainly – followed the Briton impassively, dragging or carrying his luggage and purchases, oblivious to the children who scampered around their feet.

Voices spilled from a small cafe that had seemingly been built into little more than a hole in the wall, and Saif veered closer, his attention drawn by the crackle of radio waves. A local Marrakshi station, with the receiver's mechanism badly wound. Signal noise oscillated across the frequency, and the jarring sound of somebody cranking the handle bit across the voices. Local or not, the talking point was still the same.

"Cover the whole city!" one man said, punctuating his words with sharp jabbing gestures. "That would stop them looking down!"

"Why would they want to look at us anyway?" another asked. "We have nothing to hide. Only in Europe do people have anything to hide. They should be worried, not us."

"It is a blasphemy," said the presenter

on the radio. "Only God can look down upon the Earth."

Saif hurried on. He had no time to waste this morning. The conversation reminded him of the importance of today's tasks.

The street cut through several of the city's souks, and the stalls were crowded with the morning traffic – perfect for his purposes. As he walked briskly towards the Djemaa el Fna he pulled a fresh red shirt from his satchel and shrugged it on over the top of his white vest. Next came the black skullcap and the square-rimmed glasses. Finally he changed his walk, exactly as he had been taught; longer, loping steps, with a noticeable swagger.

In less than a minute he had become a different man. Anyone who had been trying to follow him, if they had not already lost him in the bustle of the souks, should now have been thoroughly frustrated.

The Djemaa el Fna was relatively quiet, once Saif had emerged from the souks themselves. The storytellers over in the far corner had smaller audiences than usual, and there didn't seem to be as many tourists wandering across the square. One of the monkey-handlers was desperate enough for trade to approach Saif himself, and he had to skip aside neatly to avoid losing his purse to a small flea-ridden primate.

What little movement there was in the square ground to a halt at a low droning sound that seemed to come from the north, drowning out even the calls of the stall-hawkers. Saif joined everybody else in craning his head to find the source of the drone, aware of the prickle of anxiety at the back of his mind.

Sputnik – the Russians are coming – it'll fall on our heads – quickly, get everybody indoors

Before that anxiety could become full-blown panic, the dirigible appeared, scudding over the Medina at an extraordinarily low height. Saif could even see the passengers standing at the rail that ran around the airship's fuselage, tourists staring agog down at the teeming maze of the city – *so unlike the beautiful and graceful buildings of Paris, my dear! Oh, but I do hope that the hotel has hot running water...*

The square seemed to breathe

a collective sigh of relief. It wasn't the Russian spaceship. Saif knew, intellectually, that the Sputnik device would be best viewed through a telescope, and it certainly wouldn't be passing over Marrakesh at a mere few hundred feet, but his heart had thumped as fast as everybody else's.

It was a measure of how the world had changed, how shocking the very thought was that the Russians had conquered space. What would they do next? Would they demand the world's surrender from up on high? It was no wonder the rest of the world was, to say the very least, jittery about the future.

He squinted upward at the dirigible and made out the crest and flag painted on the fuselage. Sure enough, it was the

Jane Grey. That gave him twenty minutes or so before the ship was secured at Marrakesh-Menara Airport. He'd have to hurry.

The dirigible banked away to avoid the Koutoubia, and Saif changed direction himself and headed for Sharia Mohammad, where the taxis sat in long, disordered ranks, their drivers lingering in the shade of the palms by the roadside, wreathed in cigarette smoke. A party of small boys clambered over the vehicles like monkeys: they polished the mirrors and pushed dirt from the windows with filthy rags, and wound up the clacking mechanisms in twos and threes, faces twisting with the effort at some of the older, more decrepit taxis.

Saif walked along the rank until he

found the *grand* taxi he was looking for. This one was wound already, and the driver leaned against the door, waving away the children whenever they dared approach. He spat onto the ground as Saif arrived, then grinned at him.

"You're cutting it fine today," he said. "The traffic's a bitch in Gueliz. And the police are as sympathetic as pregnant donkeys."

Saif shrugged. "I'll still make it."

"Do you want one of the boys?"

He shook his head. "A kind offer, Hassan, but this one is... delicate."

Hassan tapped the side of his oft-broken nose. "Ah. And you have no time to discuss the premium now."

Saif popped the driver's door and

climbed in. The leather seats were already baking, even through the blankets that Hassan had covered them with. "I'm sure we can come to some agreement later, Hassan."

The driver threw up his arms in mock disgust. "Ah, boy, you take all the fun from life!"

His borrowed *grand* taxi was something of a beast to drive. A fault with the steering meant it tended to the left and so needed constant correction, while fourth gear was intermittently unavailable. But Saif was used to having to drive with such distractions. After all, the entire Marrakshi traffic system was designed to make grown men weep. At least with the *grand* taxi people were a little more likely to get out of his way, rather than the other way around.

Sounding the horn at regular intervals, and jerking at the wheel to switch lanes at every available opportunity, he was making good time, despite a snarl up by the Bab Doukkala that had spread quickly as far as Sharia Mohammad. The tradecraft that had been drummed into him meant he kept one eye ever on the mirrors, checking for any sign of pursuit. That there seemed to be none was, in its own way, more troubling than if he had spotted a Russian tail.

Pedestrians threw themselves into the road, heedless of the traffic signals, and boys and old men threw themselves at cars forced to halt long enough to attract their attention, wiping windscreens and grabbing at the ratchet mechanisms on the back of every vehicle. *I wind you up! I wind you up! Three dirhams! Two dirhams! I have children!*

That last came from a boy who could not be more than twelve years old. Saif laughed and waved him away disdainfully. The boy spat at the car as he jumped back onto the kerb, but Saif didn't have time to stop and teach him some manners.

If there was one thing Hassan's taxi was good for – and there were in fact a few, otherwise the Embassy would not have recruited him in the first place – it was the quality and endurance of the mechanisms under the hood. All things failed with time, but while Hassan's taxi looked dilapidated and unreliable, every single movement of the tightly wound engine clicked with the precision of superior engineering. It was good for three or four hours of hard driving, and Hassan boasted that he had driven to Casablanca and back without once having to stop to rewind the engine.

Saif doubted that claim, but even he had to admit that the mechanisms were superb. This had to be the only car in the city – aside from the king's own limousine, perhaps – that did not require the constant attention of a winding boy clinging precariously to the ratchet on the rear hood.

Beyond both the Medina itself and the bland concrete construction sites that made up the vast part of Gueliz, the traffic was less frenetic. Here, the roads were wider and straighter, laid down in advance for the great expansion of the city that had been promised for so long now. The Avenue de la Menara boasted dozens of exits that petered out into fenced-off squares of dusty nothing, populated by donkeys, camels and the rusted shells of cannibalised mechs.

Young palms lined the central reservation, with unemployed men clustered in groups underneath them. This was a world away from the conquest of space. But if the Russians had signalled the beginning of what many Western commentators were now calling the Space Age, then the British Empire would surely be close behind. And their scientists would need precision instruments and highly specialised equipment to manufacture their riposte to the giants of the East. Who better to make and provide these items than the one culture that understood these things best?

Saif knew the answer to that question, as did the king himself and all of his advisors. And, indeed, so did the British. Soon North Africa would be rich again, and perhaps the Avenue de la Menara would become a new, shining jewel in the Moroccan crown.

But before all of that could happen, Saif had to make sure this one mission went smoothly and according to plan. He glanced across through the windscreen and saw, in the distance, the curving bulk of the *Jane Grey* making its last descending turns over the landing pad. He was back on schedule; all he had to do was make the pick-up.

The trickle of new arrivals through the doors of the terminal became a surge of cream suits and white shirts, interspersed with the pastel shades and bright floral patterns of women's dresses and jackets. Imported mechs followed the crowd at a distance with the hard travelling cases that the tourists seemed to believe were indispensable.

Every face seemed hidden beneath a hat – wide-brimmed, beribboned or fashionable. Something that could only make Saif's first attempts at contact that much harder. He wished now that he had brought along one of Hassan's many children: at least he would have been able to leave the boy to guard the car while he ventured onto the terminal's main concourse.

He craned his neck and squinted at the crowd, cursing under his breath. Now he would end up with a meaningless fare back into the city centre, while his contact got fleeced by a regular driver.

He caught a glimpse of a man shouldering his way towards the front of the queue: short, with a slight frame and pale skin that would quickly burn a crisp red in the African sun if his fair beard was anything to judge him by. His suit looked to be at least one size too large for him, and he carried a battered old satchel that reminded Saif of his school days in Marseille. His eyes were hidden behind thick, round sunglasses, but Saif had the distinct feeling that the man was staring straight at him. Was this the contact?

Well, if they had given me some details I'd know for certain! he thought in frustration. He placed both hands on top of his head – the initial signal – and watched the man change direction and push across the flow of the crowd toward him.

"Monsieur!" Saif called out. "Twelve dirhams to the Medina!"

"Nine's a fairer price," the man said, casting his gaze along the rest of the taxi rank while he spoke. "What price to Dar Cherifa?"

That was the next part of the script. Saif allowed himself to relax a little. "Eleven dirhams, right to the very doorstep."

"Ten and it's a deal," the man replied.

"Monsieur, you are as ruthless as the Russians!"

"Aye, and twice as pretty too." The man smiled unexpectedly, revealing both a golden tooth and a considerable underbite. "Come on then, son, let's go."

He lounged in the rear of the taxi, the satchel on his lap and his arms spread over the backs of the seats, content to watch the city as though he was a tourist as Saif threaded his way back through to the Medina. Saif eyed him surreptitiously in the rear-view mirror. He didn't seem to be quite what Saif had expected.

"Your first time in the country, sir?" Saif made the question as polite as he could, to test the water.

"More or less," the man said in a manner that closed the subject as soon as it had been opened. He reached into his jacket and brought out a large leather-bound case – for his spectacles, Saif guessed. "Take a route via the Bab el Khemis, please."

Saif frowned. That was over on the far side of the Medina and would take them out of their way. But the British agent was staring at him from behind his darkened lenses, and so he nodded and pulled the car into the left-hand lane, expertly cutting up one of the city's diesel-burning coaches.

The buzzing of insects inside the taxi distracted him for a moment and he glanced around to try to identify the little beasts. A tiny glint, as if off a metallic carapace, from one corner of the windscreen, and Saif's muscles tensed. Spymoths!

"Sir..." he said, his voice cracking with urgency. "We've – "

"I know," the agent said calmly. "Just keep driving, please."

Another glance in the mirror, Saif hoping to reassure himself that the man was taking control of the situation. But he sat back, as relaxed as before, with the hardened case open on one hand.

Even as Saif watched another small shape crawled up onto the edge of the case and, wings whirring furiously into life, leapt into the air. Saif cringed and chewed his lip, waiting for the prickling sensation of a spymoth's poisonous bite. At least there wouldn't be too much after that.

He thought – or maybe he imagined it – he heard a small crunch from somewhere inside the taxi. Then the British agent chuckled to himself. "You can relax now, son. We can talk."

The buzzing continued, though now it seemed a little quieter. Saif thought that the spymoths might be underneath the seats. Even now one might be crawling on his shoe. He fought the temptation to shake his legs, in case he angered the single-minded insects.

"But... spymoths, sir? Aren't we in danger?"

The man shook his head. "Christ, no. Not from them, anyhow. These are special issue. Bug-hunters."

Saif nearly forgot to make the next turn. "Bug-hunters? The taxi is bugged? By who – the Chinese, sir?" He'd heard rumours that the British had managed to duplicate some of the older spymoth technology from the Chinese – the undoubted masters in that field – but the bugs themselves still defied any attempt at duplication. The Caliphate was even further behind in that particular race, Saif knew. But why would the Chinese want in on this deal? What kind of information might be at stake?

The British agent had picked something

up from the floor of the taxi, and now held it close to his face, turning it in his hand. "Hmm. No, I don't think so. That's worrying. Keep going for the Bab el Khemis: we'll dump the car there and carry on through the souks on foot."

Saif winced. The taxi would be stripped or stolen within the hour. Hassan would not be pleased about this.

The man stretched a thick, well-manicured hand between the front seats. "Foxwood, S.F.O. Pleased to meet you."

Saif shook his hand uncertainly. This wasn't happening quite the way it should have done. "What's going on, sir? We got told you were here for an important pick-up, and the meeting has been set up – but we've been getting some really heavy notes from the Russians over the last few days."

Foxwood nodded his head upwards. "And all of that up there didn't tip you off at all? Disappointing, son. Disappointing."

Saif checked his mirrors again, reminded that the Russians had reinforced their North African contingents over the last few weeks. Foxwood was intimating that this was all because of the Sputnik. And more besides: that this visit to Marrakesh had something to do with the Russian space programme.

The spymoths stopped humming at last. With no other bugs found in the taxi they had returned to Foxwood's leather-bound case. He dropped it back into his pocket with a satisfied smile. "That'll flummox them for a while. Probably not long enough, unfortunately, but one can't have everything."

Saif just nodded weakly.

"How's the Old Man?" Foxwood continued, much more relaxed now that the taxi's interior was secure. "Still scything everybody's feet off at the ankles?"

The regional head of the Caliphate's Directorate of Security, Mohammed el-Fadil, was a veteran of Morocco's armed forces. Badly injured during the Saharan skirmishes that had preceded the Second World War, he had been retired to the bureaucracy. But with the aid of British-built pneumatics and Marrakshi engineering, he had soon become mobile again, and now clattered about his headquarters on a variety of contraptions that could be lethally injurious to anyone careless enough not to listen for his approach. Saif himself had been bruised and bowled over several times before he learned to keep to the sides of the corridors.

He tried to suppress a grin. "We call him the Engine. Not to his face, of course."

"Of course not," Foxwood agreed. "Now, where and when is the handover scheduled? Just in case we have any more trouble."

"A safe house behind the Café Marrakesh," Saif said. "A red door with three diagonal scratches. Knock and ask for Señor Castillo." The information had been passed to him just a few minutes before he left his own safe house in the Medina; there was no way it could have been compromised this quickly by the Russians. Unless they got their bugs into us too. The thought slipped into his mind and lodged there like an unwanted fever.

Another mirror check, this one fuelled by a growing paranoia. A dusty, diesel-engined saloon slid into his eye-line and he realised with a shudder that he had seen it once already today. Bulky silhouettes occupied the seats behind the dirty windscreen. Three vehicles back: Saif gunned the accelerator and overtook some of the traffic ahead, ignoring the frenzied cacophony of horns that complained in his wake. Now he looked back again – the saloon was still there, three vehicles back.

"Dogs' cocks!" he swore, angry at his failure to spot the tail earlier. This was no way to impress a man of Foxwood's quality.

The British agent leaned forward and tried to use the rear-view mirror. "We have a tail? Hah – no surprise there, son. Right. Where are we?"

"Back near Bab Doukkala, sir," Saif replied.

"Excellent. Time for a bracing constitutional! Pull in at the square, son. And don't hang around."

The square before Bab Doukkala was where tradesmen had traditionally waited to be picked for whatever labour needed doing, whether it was bricklaying, plastering, carpentry, or even unskilled ground clearance. They sat in groups, with the tools of their trades displayed at their feet, smoking, drinking and playing dice until after the sun went down. These days they had been joined by sub-contractors, with ranks of R-mechs in various states of disrepair. There could be a lot of ill-feeling between the workers and the sub-contractors, especially when work was scarce.

Saif swerved across three lanes of traffic and drove the *grand* taxi up the kerb and onto the large area of open ground outside the Bab Doukkala, causing pigeons and pedestrians alike to scatter from the area. He didn't wait for the taxi to stop, simply opening the door and throwing himself onto the stone, with a red flare of pain as his shoulder hit the ground. He rolled, exactly as he had been taught, and felt another sharp stab in his side as he knocked into a small pile of masonry trowels that one cluster of men had been forced to abandon.

Adrenalin brought him quickly back to his feet. He staggered into a run, heedless of the taxi which was careering toward the wall of the Medina. He could see Foxwood up ahead: the older man strode with dignified but obvious alacrity in the same direction, half-turned to cover his retreat, apparently not fazed in the slightest by his rushed dive from the cab. He had abandoned his satchel somewhere, but there was a small revolver in one hand.

Further commotion behind him caused Saif to hurry his own pace. He glanced over his shoulder to see the pursuing saloon skewed against the kerb, disgorging men and thick-limbed mechs into the square. The police were going to have a field day with this incident, he thought.

Hassan's taxi hit the wall a few yards from the Bab Doukkala and the chassis crunched and concertinaed. The engine clacked with an ugly, hurried sound, cogs displaced and flying out from under the hood as it unwound violently.

"Hurry up!" Foxwood shouted, gesturing at him. "It's on a timer!"

Saif didn't understand what he meant, but he lowered his head and pushed himself toward the gate, where a large number of the square's crowd had retreated. A pair of sharp cracks signalled the Russian agents' sudden escalation of the situation. Saif wished he had a weapon so that he could return fire himself, but el-Fadil's current orders precluded anything that could be seen as provocative to either the Russians or the British Empire.

Foxwood, on the other hand, had no such compunctions. As he reached the gate's arch he turned and snapped off three quick shots at the Russians. Saif skidded through the gate just as another round ricocheted off the corner of the arch. "Right, sir! Let's go – they have mechs!"

"Hah," Foxwood sniffed. But he followed Saif at a brisk trot and they veered left, over the road and past the drains that were used as open urinals, and into the side streets of the Medina.

The air became thick for a brief

moment, and then the shockwave of the explosion made Saif stumble, unbalanced by his sudden deafness. Now he knew what had happened to Foxwood's satchel.

"That'll keep 'em busy for a while," Foxwood judged with a hard smile. He was quite unnerving, Saif decided. He was glad the man's eyes were hidden behind his sunglasses. "Now then: the Café Marrakesh, I think you said. And don't hurry – we don't need to draw attention upon ourselves, do we?"

The square in front of the café was a minor reflection of the Djemaa el Fna: spice traders and pot sellers clogged the space in the middle, while tourists dodged between darkened shopfronts and compared carpets and teapots. The café itself was a grander affair, as though it had been transplanted from the Red Square only half a mile away; three storeys high, the roof had been converted to a relaxing and shaded garden, complete with decorative rails that its more salubrious clientèle could lean upon while sipping their small glasses of mint tea.

That balcony looked rather crowded when Saif entered the square, his ears still ringing and his nerves upset by the explosion that had ripped across the Bab Doukkala. He had dumped his shirt and hat along the way to change his appearance once more; Foxwood still wore his big cream suit, but so many other men followed the same fashion that he seemed to blend in.

Saif would normally have avoided the café altogether – there was a faster route to the safe house through the alleyway he had mentioned to Foxwood earlier – but the abrupt and violent turn of events made him want to put a few more obstacles between himself and the Russians, even if they were hampered by the explosives left inside Hassan's taxi.

He took the steps quickly, muttering an apology to the expensively dressed Germans who were coming the other way, and strode through the interior toward the kitchens, flashing a few quick hand signals to the nondescript agents who habitually used one of the window seats as a guard post.

Foxwood plucked a handwritten menu from the basket that hung by the door as he entered, glancing about the place as if he was himself an ordinary tourist, being shown around the Medina by a hired guide. Even in the relative gloom of the café – it was nearing noon and most people were now retreating indoors to escape the withering heat – he wore his opaque-looking sunglasses.

The café's proprietor intercepted Saif before he reached the kitchens, a worried frown deepening the lines on his face. "Was that your lot?" he asked bluntly. Saif didn't need to wonder what he meant. Sometimes word travelled faster than sound itself.

He shrugged. "Technically, no," he said. "But we do need to come through to the yard."

The proprietor eyed Foxwood suspiciously. "Oh, of course. Very unobtrusive, I must say." He raised a warning finger under Saif's nose. "There had better not be any trouble from this. I run a respectable business, you know."

It was the same every time, but on this occasion Saif could easily resist the urge to grin at him. "I'll let the boss know."

The proprietor stepped aside. "And so will I."

They dodged through the kitchens and into the dirty alley behind the café. This was a side of the old city that most visitors never saw. Small hovels almost hanging from the uneven walls of the buildings, vermin darting in and out of the piles of festering rubbish, half-clothed children staring up in wonder at the visitors who flitted through their world like gods. Smoke, tainted with the sickly tang of hashish, permeated the air; a far cry from the refined environs of the Café Marrakesh only a wall's breadth away.

Saif glanced over his shoulder to check Foxwood's reaction, but the slender agent seemed unfazed by the squalor.

The buzzing of insects made him flinch for a moment until he realised that the sound did not have the metallic chittering so characteristic of the spymoths. These were just flies, disturbed from rest by his passing. He sighed and forced himself to relax. The safe house wasn't far now.

"I suppose I should be glad we aren't

going to the place in the tanneries," Foxwood muttered, staring down at a smear on his sleeve. "Had I known, I most definitely would not have worn cream."

Beyond this alley, which didn't even warrant the name of a derb, the way was a little clearer. The upper storeys of the buildings leaned toward each other, conspiring to hide the path entirely from daylight. Families and passers-by made the most of the shade, squatting in corners with drinks and pipes. The tantalising smell of slow-cooking tagines came from niches and small windows, reminding Saif that he was hungry.

Even the mechs, ever-present in the more accessible parts of the Medina, had not made it this far. These were the poor districts, home to those who might have been displaced by the mechanical workers. Some of the men were skilled metalworkers; they might one day find work if the Caliphate's economic plans ever came to fruition, but meanwhile the mechs were constant and reliable and squeezed the artisans to the periphery.

Saif was so intent on his path between the many obstacles, half his attention distracted by the possibility of pursuit, that he almost missed the safe house's entrance. He wheeled about just in time and rapped the code on the door.

Foxwood came to a halt and stared around, still apparently in the role of an imperious traveller, oblivious to all dangers. Saif noted, however, that the British agent had braced his hands firmly on his hips, under his jacket, and that the holster under his armpit was unbuckled.

A shutter in the door snapped open and Saif found himself meeting a narrow and suspicious gaze. "Yes? Who is it?"

"It's me, uncle!" Saif raised his voice. "I brought the doctor for Señor Castillo!"

"Phah. You took your time, idiot." The shutter slammed closed again. Locks thudded back and the door creaked open. Saif ducked under the lintel and into the gloomy interior. The tiny hallway beyond turned immediately to the left, then dog-legged back upon itself, down a few steps into the house's central courtyard. Sunlight bloomed down upon him; it felt like hours since he had last felt it on his skin, rather than only a few minutes.

Matif was waiting for them, barely restraining his impatience as he perched on one of the wicker chairs laid out in the courtyard. Others sat in a group on the cushions in one of the shaded quarters. A domestic mech hummed on a balcony that encircled the first floor, polishing the rails methodically, ignoring everything that happened around it.

Matif glared down his nose. "At last! What on earth is going on out there? Do you have any idea of the trouble you have caused?"

Saif stepped aside quickly, his hands raised in self-defence. "Sir! I followed all the directions completely!"

The deputy chief of the security directorate cast him a withering glance. "Not you, boy. *Him*." He turned back to Foxwood, who wore a lazy smile as he dusted off his jacket. "Shots fired? Explosives? It's a miracle nobody was seriously hurt out there, let alone the damage this has done to our relations with the Russians!"

"They fired first," Foxwood said, as though this explained everything. "We did warn you that this was highly sensitive information: they weren't likely to let us have it without a fight."

"And thus, they send us Foxwood the lightning rod," Matif snapped. "The one man guaranteed to make a hard situation even harder. Not difficult to tell that you studied under 'Biffy' Dunderdale."

The British agent shrugged. "There wasn't anybody else available. Would you believe it? Biggest job so far this century

– just look what the damn Russians have thrown up there – and the whole bloody department was completely wrong-footed. Who would you want to entrust this mission to, eh? Everett? He's too green by half; doesn't know his way around the field. Canning? The man's a damned clerk – got his head in the clouds all day."

"Irrelevant," a new voice said from behind Saif. He stepped aside again to allow the man past. A Sikh, in an expensively understated suit – most probably Saville Row; the cut was excellent and emphasised his height. He looked exhausted, but his gaze was sharper than any Berber's knife. "What matters is the exit route and the completion of the contract. It matters not what happens after that."

Foxwood tilted his head back to stare up at the man. "Agreed. And the faster we do that, the faster we can all get out of here and tell the Russians this never happened. I've got a tennis match promised for this weekend."

The Sikh smiled. "We do not wish to inconvenience you, Mr Foxwood. Follow me, please."

Unsure whether he was meant to be included in this invitation, Saif tagged on nervously to the back of the group as the Sikh led the way to the shaded anteroom. He stopped by the doorway, held back by Matif's discreet but firm touch.

Foxwood tipped the brim of his hat in a gesture of courtesy and bowed slightly to the woman who sat, wilting like an unwatered flower, on the cushions against one wall. "Ah, this must be the young lady in question. Miss Zakopalova, am I correct? A pleasure to make your acquaintance, I must say."

By craning his head to one side Saif found himself with a far better view. This young woman, the apparent cause of all this trouble, seemed to be little more than a girl, perhaps the same age as Saif himself. A thick woollen robe, similar to those the Berbers still wore, was draped over her shoulders. Underneath that she wore a dull skirt and a white blouse, both stained by days of arduous travel.

While the Sikh had clearly found the opportunity to clean and refresh himself beforehand, the woman's hair was lank and matted and her face was smeared with dirt. Moreover, a thick bandage had been wrapped around the left half of her head to cover her eye – a serious injury, Saif decided. The poor girl would never be beautiful.

She said something, so quietly that Saif could not make out the words. Foxwood bent on one knee and carefully lifted up the bandage, peering underneath with such solicitousness that he might have been a surgeon. "I see," he said at length. "Oh yes, I see. Such ingenuity. And such bravery too," he added. "I shall never underestimate the courage of the fairer sex."

The Sikh cleared his throat politely. "We apologise for the delay, Mr Foxwood. The original plan, as you well know, was to make use of the North Passage. But the weather was against us and did not look set to change. And since we were told that a direct run into Europe would have met with severe resistance, we had to make alternative arrangements."

Foxwood stood again, now all business. "The North Passage would have been suicide," he said. "Even we don't know what's going on up there. The Colonel's up to his neck in it. And as for the more direct routes – Fleming's convinced we've got a leak over in the Eastern Med, even though Philby's spent months looking for it. We didn't dare bring you over that way."

The Sikh shrugged. "Crossing Afghanistan was the easy part," he said. "Once we regained Indian territory the Russians were never more than two steps behind us, even after we took working passage on a steamer around the Cape to throw them off our scent. Crossing the Atlas Mountains, in in hindsight, may have been one diversion too many."

The British agent was still staring down at the girl. "Better late than never," he commented. "Even though they pulled their ace on us in the meantime, we got what we wanted in the end."

The Sikh scratched one ear. "Is that the official position of the British Government, Mr Foxwood?"

Foxwood nodded. "Oh, aye. His Majesty greatly appreciates the efforts you've been put to."

"Then it is our pleasure to serve," the Sikh replied, drawing himself up smartly. Saif found himself being pulled back out into the courtyard by Matif, recognising belatedly that this was the private, business end of the deal.

Matif took him to the opposite side of the house, where a tray with two short glasses and a teapot sat on a low table. In the room beyond, a half dozen Marrakshi agents were co-ordinating the efforts to round up and pacify the Russians and mop up the mess in front of the Bab Doukkala. From their hushed but frantic tones, Saif guessed it was not an easy task.

"Did you have to destroy the taxi?" Matif asked as he poured the tea. Hassan was a cousin, or a nephew, or some such relation, Saif remembered. Just to make things more complicated, Saif himself was related, though his mother's family, to the deputy chief.

"Um, that was Mr Foxwood's doing, sir," Saif said hastily. "He insisted we abandon the car; I honestly was not aware that he had brought explosives with him."

Matif sighed. "Of course not – you have never dealt with the damned man before, after all. Let that be a lesson then. Perhaps for us all."

Saif could not hide his curiosity. "Sir? Who is the woman? And why do the Russians want her?"

Matif regarded him from under heavy eyelids for a moment, as though weighing his trustworthiness. At last he shrugged; a minute, perhaps even subconscious, gesture. "Svetlana Zakopalova is – was

– a secretary to one of the generals in charge of the Russian space-flight programme. For the last three years she has also been one of most secret and deeply hidden British espionage agents. Her family suffered greatly at Russian hands during the First World War, and the British found her an easy target, especially when her brother, a test pilot of experimental aircraft, was killed in a botched operation that was poorly covered up. Unfortunately, her cover was so deep, and she was so well-placed, that transmission or retrieval of any sensitive information was almost impossible. Until now."

"What changed, sir?"

He nodded up at the clear midday sky. "The Sputnik. Svetlana broke cover to report that the Russians were not only readying the launch of that damned satellite, but that they were months away from launching a man into space. The British were appalled – by all accounts they are still some way behind in that race. They have pulled the girl out, along with all the information she could bring with her, in the hope that they can pull themselves ahead of the Russians. Naturally, the Russians do not want that information handed over." He ventured a wry smile. "The fact that Miss Zakopalova torched the original files after copying them appears to have inflamed the situation."

He sipped his tea and looked back at the other side of the courtyard, where Foxwood and the Sikh remained deep in conversation. "A brave young girl. If they were all like that, perhaps we would now all write in Cyrillic lettering."

One of the agents called out to him and Matif hurried over, leaving Saif with his tea. He'd had no idea of the scale of this mission, he mused, walking slowly along the colonnade toward the house's kitchens. The stakes involved were truly enormous. No wonder the Caliphate had decided to come down on the British side. The Russians were unlikely to ever include them in any construction or technology projects for the new space rockets.

He stopped by a flower bed and tipped the leafy dregs into it. A few bees floated erratically around the roses, drawn by the pollen, and he took care to avoid disturbing them. Circling the flowers as agents circled information, he thought, pleased with the metaphor.

One of the bees looked larger, flying in jagged lines as though angered. It veered straight at Saif and he jerked aside just in time, wondering at its belligerence. At the corner of his vision he saw Matif stiffen and raise a hand to his face, crying out in sudden pain. Another agent grabbed at a sheaf of papers and waved them in the air, batting at something unseen.

Not bees. Wasps. Spywasps. The Russians were deeper in bed with the Chinese than even el-Fadil had thought.

"The girl!" Matif shouted at him. His face glowed, as if it had been slapped. "Get her out!"

Even as Saif launched into a run, he saw Foxwood casting about for something to use as a weapon against the insects. The Sikh, meanwhile, as exhausted as he had to be, had reacted even faster, ripping a patterned throw from a low couch and covering the Russian defector with it, heedless of his own safety.

"Get us to a door!" Foxwood ordered. "*Is* there a back door?"

Saif pointed to a narrow doorway at the back of the anteroom, where steps led away to the kitchen. "This way, sir!"

He led the way, while Foxwood and the Sikh bundled Zakopalova between them. The British agent swiped at the air with his hat, fending off as many of the wasps' attacks as he could, but the Sikh had clearly been stung already – his face was twisted in a grimace and he made little effort to defend himself.

As he reached the arch that led down into the kitchen, Saif saw that the door beyond, which led into another dingy alleyway, was being cut open from outside – jagged lines crossed the wood where razor-sharp saw-arms sliced through it. They had only seconds before the door collapsed completely.

"Mechs!" he shouted over his shoulder. "They're coming through!"

The sound of gunfire echoed down the hall from the main courtyard. "And that's the front door blocked as well," Foxwood noted.

Saif cast about urgently. "The stairs – to the roof!"

The stairwells of these old houses were awkward at the best of times: taking the steep flights two or three at a time, pulling the shrouded and exhausted Svetlana Zakopalova after him, and stumbling heavily against the stone to bruise his palms and shins, Saif reflected that these were definitely not the best of times.

The crack of Foxwood's revolver came from below, just around the turn of the stair; the Sikh, apparently overcome by the toxins of the spywasps' stings, was no longer with them.

Saif passed the landing to the first floor and caught sight of the mech that was still cleaning the balcony railings. "There's a mess downstairs!" he shouted to it. "Code Sparta-Alpha – clean it up!"

The mech jerked upright and headed for the stairwell with renewed purpose. Now it would seek to remove all intruders it came across, by any means necessary, until either the house was cleared, or the mech itself was destroyed. Saif could only hope that somebody had managed to issue the same orders to the mechs that worked downstairs; at least it would buy them a little time. He was under no illusions that they could defeat a determined Russian force – they had neither the skills nor the brutal technology to pit against them.

"Come on," he urged Zakopalova. "We have to run!"

She sobbed and said something that he could not understand, but her hand snaked out from beneath the throw to grasp his tightly, and he pulled her along the landing to the next set of stairs. A quick glance behind him revealed Foxwood backing onto the landing, expelling spent cartridges from his revolver.

Bullets ricocheted off the white plastered walls by Saif's head. It seemed that the Russians did not need their quarry alive. He ducked into the stairwell and began to pray that the roof was clear.

"Faster, boy!" Foxwood roared from behind them. "My old grandmother could beat you up those stairs!"

"She never said you'd be this rude!" he spat back. A poor effort, but it earned a sharp bark of laughter from the man.

"That's the spirit! We're not done for yet!"

Saif gained the rooftop garden. The spywasps had been up here already – the two guards Matif had set both lay motionless on the tiled floor that encircled the roof, their faces purpled and their hands outstretched in clawed desperation. Saif tugged the girl out of the stairwell and stooped to pick up the hat that one of the guards had worn. If there were still any of the damned insects hovering about the garden he would at least have something with which to defend himself.

Foxwood appeared and pulled the door shut, cursing the fact that he could not lock it from the outside. "Are you both alright?" he asked, the heaviness of his breathing the sole indication that he had been put to work.

Saif had managed to avoid the

spywasps, unlike the poor Sikh, who now probably lay sprawled on the stairs. He lifted the throw from Svetlana's head and the girl gasped in fresh air gratefully. The bandage over the left side of her face had slipped very slightly, but other than that she too seemed unharmed.

"Good. So far, so good," Foxwood muttered, in direct contradiction of the evidence that their situation offered. "Now for the interesting part, I suppose."

"Another bracing constitutional, sir?" Saif asked, listening for any sign of movement on the stairwell below.

Foxwood smiled. "Just a shame I seem to have run out of explosives, son. Now then – where are the planks?"

Saif pointed wordlessly to a long

alcove under one wall, where a half-dozen scaffolding planks sat sheltered against rain and sunlight alike. The British agent hurried over and began to pull out the planks one by one. He thrust the first across the tiles toward Saif. "Come on then, boy, get a move on. We haven't got all day. Get the girl across; I'll follow."

Saif heaved the heavy plank into the air and let it drop outward over the house's far wall. It thumped onto the roof on the other side of the narrow alley. He urged the Russian girl up onto the plank. "Don't worry, it's perfectly safe. I'm right behind you."

If she understood at all she said nothing to him in reply, but she scrambled out across the divide with no hesitation. The plank bowed under her weight but held solid. Saif watched her drop safely onto the other side and then hauled himself up to follow. A hoarse whistle made him pause, snapping his head back to look at Foxwood: the agent tossed his spectacles case underarm across the roof, and Saif caught it one-handed. He tucked it quickly into his pocket as the agent's revolver followed close behind.

"Sir? You'll need this, surely?"

Foxwood shook his head with a smile. "I have other tricks up my sleeve." He gestured Saif away. "Go, boy. The *Jane Grey*'s waiting."

The gun was an unfamiliar weight in his hand, and he struggled to keep his balance as he took the makeshift bridge in three long strides. Svetlana

Zakopalova stared at him warily, and then her monocular gaze shifted back over his shoulder.

"He'll find us," Saif said. He heard gunshots again, echoing up from the well of the safehouse's courtyard. "Look, we have to keep moving. Please, miss?"

She exhaled and suddenly the exhaustion was plain upon her face once more: she must have been running for weeks now, Saif realised, every fibre of her being stretched and tested beyond the limits of human endurance. He wondered how much further she could possibly run.

"Da," she said, motioning Saif to lead on.

The Directorate had set up several roof-runs that took direct paths over the Medina, stretching out across the quiet gardens and messy shanties in a web of scaffold boards and discreet ramps. Even from the skies an observer might not notice the routes they took, unless he already knew what to look for.

Saif ran with the borrowed gun stuck through his belt, his hands free so that he could upset and topple the bridges once they had passed over. The boards fell into unminded alleyways, or were pulled back across where they bridged busier streets – he had no intention of causing innocent casualties.

Zakopalova followed his directions almost wordlessly, even when he forgot to point the way forward; it was clear to him that she understood at least some English. On more than one occasion she doubled back to help him withdraw a bridge, stubbornly and deliberately mishearing his protests.

At least there was no immediate sign of pursuit, Saif thought, but given the intelligence and efficiency the Russians had shown so far, that didn't mean as much as it ought to have done. For all he knew the Russians might be tracking them from the streets. He resisted the temptation to stop and watch over the side of the roof to see whether he was right. Indecision and hesitation were a man's worst enemies, el-Fadil had taught him.

He scanned the skyline. The Koutoubbia was over *there*, so Gueliz and the Bab Doukkala were over *there*. He had a choice between making for the gate, which was closer and undoubtedly much faster, or for the Sharia Mohammed again, where he would be able to pick up transport and a few escorts.

As he caught his breath the call to prayer sounded. Speakers atop the Koutoubbia started the cry, and it was taken up quickly by the mosques in the surrounding districts. Saif ducked his head in a quick obeisance and directed a prayer to the heavens.

The thrumming vibration of Foxwood's spectacles case against his hip took him by surprise and he tugged it from his pocket in alarm, half-expecting it to explode in his face. Given Foxwood's actions today he wouldn't have put that past the man. This was the case that housed the agent's spymoths, he remembered – what could agitate them so much that they would do this?

Svetlana frowned back at him and grabbed his sleeve, trying to urge him onward again. He pulled himself free and jogged across the roof behind her, fiddling with the clasp that held the case closed.

Svetlana ducked and shouted suddenly, and then Saif heard the buzzing at last. Russian spywasps – they had been found! Something buzzed past his ear as he closed the distance to join Svetlana at the edge of the roof, and he flinched, jerking to one side instinctively.

"Onto the street!" he told her, turning on the spot in a desperate effort to locate the lethal insectoids. "They can be confused down there."

Svetlana nodded and swung her legs over the side of the roof without hesitation. There was a rickety wooden ladder that led down into an alleyway in the middle of one of the souks and she descended it with ease. Saif made to follow, then hesitated – the case was vibrating even harder than before. He popped it open and threw it away from him with the same motion, flinging up one arm to cover his face just in case it did explode. He caught a glimpse of the spymoths whirring up into the sky, and then they split away, dancing in patterns he could not follow, chasing the Russian wasps.

Elatedly thanking God, he swung onto the ladder. From here the easiest way was probably towards the Sharia Mohammed. The souks would shield them both from any further attacks by Russian spywasps. Deadly they might be, but they were quite useless in large crowds, unable to discriminate their targets from innocents.

"Are you all right, miss?" he gasped as he caught up with the girl.

She looked shaken, but he could not see the flush that signalled the presence of the fast-working toxins the Russians preferred. "Da. Yes. Quickly, please."

He smiled despite his own exhaustion. "Da. No problem, miss."

The Djemaa el-Fna was a lot busier now. The first of the afternoon's outdoor restaurants was being set up speedily in one corner, and the carts that held the evening's fresh produce and the frames of the stalls, kitchens and tables had gathered along several of the roads that led into the square. The mechs had intruded even into this part of daily life: they pulled the carts without question, and constructed the frames methodically and single-mindedly, displacing the old men for whom this task was a major part of their day.

Saif squeezed his way through the crowds, warding off the street traders who seemed to home in unerringly on Svetlana. It didn't help that she looked around with a wild gaze, stumbling across the square as though lost or ill. After the third occasion that he had to double back and rescue her from a man insistently trying to sell her trinkets for good luck, he pulled her along behind him instead, heedless of how obvious they might appear to their pursuers.

"How far now?" she called out to him. "My feet...!"

"Not far!" he managed between breaths. "We can get a car!"

Hassan was nowhere in sight, thankfully. Saif thought that the news of his taxi's destruction must have reached him by now, and he would be mourning, desolate, over the ruined pieces. Saif searched up and down the rank of taxis quickly, trying to work out which of the old vehicles was the least unreliable; which would probably not need re-winding before they reached the airport.

Svetlana pulled at his hand. "Too long! They come!"

He didn't want to wait around to test the truth of that: he allowed her to dive into the front passenger seat of the nearest *grand* taxi and scooted into the back himself. The driver, half-asleep, jerked awake with a cry of alarm, raising his hands in self-defence. "I have no money!"

"Never mind that," Saif said. "Get us to the airport in five minutes and we'll pay you triple."

The driver twisted about in his seat and finally saw who had invaded his taxi. "You – you? Ah, a curse on you and your secret agents!"

Svetlana uttered an impatient curse

in Russian, and her words rose into a scream as something smashed into the window next to her. Saif caught a glimpse of a thick steel body on the pavement outside. The mech reached in through the broken window and grabbed for Svetlana's shoulder. She cried out and dived across to the other side of the car, which had been swiftly vacated by the panicked driver. Saif drew the revolver and fired two shots off at the mech. The bullets ricocheted, sparking, from the body.

Svetlana gunned the engine; the gears crunched and the taxi roared forward. Saif lost his balance and fell hard against the front seats, losing his grip on the revolver. He found himself jammed into the footwell, broken glass pricking his arm.

Metal clashed on metal, screeching as the taxi rebounded against the other traffic on the road. Irregular clanking from underneath the car told Saif that all was not well with the complex gearing systems that drove the vehicle.

"Shit! Shit!" Svetlana Zakopalova spat. Saif hauled himself back up, his muscles straining with the effort, and saw that the taxi was veering from side to side; she was struggling with the steering. "Piece of shit car!"

Her English wasn't so bad after all, Saif thought.

They careered off another vehicle, forcing it into the next lane. The resulting pile-up was an inevitable chain reaction. While he scrabbled in the footwell with one hand, searching for the gun, Saif craned his head to look for pursuit. This was all wrong, he realised – he should be in the front seat, taking the girl away from danger. It was little wonder he felt so unbalanced.

He braced himself for yet another impact. "Watch out – drive straighter!"

Svetlana swung her head and glared at him. "I have one eye! One eye!" And she stared back through the dirty windscreen, concentrating furiously on the road despite her lack of depth of vision.

"Then let me drive!" Saif argued.

She spared one hand for a quick dismissive wave. "No time. Shit! Shit car!"

The Russian accent gave her profanities a distinctive and somewhat suitable edge, even if it was odd to hear the words coming from a woman who he thought should have been the epitome of Russian glacial calm. Saif grinned as he flung himself onto the seat behind her.

"Tell me where," Svetlana ordered.

He took his bearings quickly. "Left. Then straight." It was only now that he thought to check the road behind them for pursuit. The rear window was so filthy it was a miracle he could see through it at all, but he managed to spot the looming shapes of the mechs on the paving far behind them. There was a disturbance in the traffic back there too – *another* disturbance, he amended his thought silently, since Svetlana'a driving had already caused chaos on the road – and that had to be the Russians.

It was all down to speed now. Speed,

and an unhealthy dose of luck.

"They're coming after us," he said.

Svetlana said nothing to that, but she did curse under her breath as the taxi narrowly avoided sideswiping a bus. With no peripheral vision on that side another collision was only a matter of time.

"What happened to your eye?" He couldn't resist the question.

"Accident," she snapped. For a moment Saif thought she would say nothing more, but then she glanced over her shoulder at him for a second, as if judging her words. "Travel to Alexandria after Pavel dead. Car crash. Doctors work for British – make new eye."

"Is it damaged?"

Svetlana shook her head. "No. *Full.*"

She thumped the steering wheel with both hands. "Shit car! Slow!"

Saif realised with alarm that traffic was passing them on both sides – the *grand* taxi appeared to be slowing down. The vibrations of the gearing underneath him told the same story. "Oh, dogs' cocks!"

He didn't believe he could move so fast: with the revolver now found and tucked once more into his belt, he grabbed the winding key from its rest behind the driver's seat and used it to smash the rear window. Glass sprayed across the interior of the taxi; heedless, he scrambled up so that he was halfway out of the window and slapped the key down onto the taxi's winding mechanism.

"Keep going!" he shouted back down at the young woman. "But take it easy

– try not to hit anything!"

Whatever obscenity she shouted in return was lost in the piercing blare of car horns. Saif braced himself in place as best he could and began to wind. It was something he'd not had to do himself for many years now; not since Matif had taken him under his wing. The resistance of the mechanism pulled hard at his muscles. It seemed to take forever just to complete a single turn, and many more would be needed yet to keep the taxi moving.

"God give me strength," he gasped, shifting his hands for a better grip. It didn't get any easier: the waifs and strays who offered their services on the roads had to own the strength of men three times their size.

He raised his head for a moment and saw another taxi, further back, trying to bully its way through the traffic. The Russians would be upon them in less than a minute. He had to make a decision: abandon the car now and take a chance on gaining better transport before they were caught, or trust that he could give the car enough wound-up tension to give them the momentum to reach the airport.

Saif pushed himself fully out onto the hood of the car and put his whole weight behind the crank. The ratchet, rusted through years of poor maintenance, creaked in protest and then began to rattle like an automatic weapon, unoiled cogs jarring Saif's arms. Round and around and around and around – suddenly the mechanism had freed itself up, as though God himself had heard his prayer.

For a long agonising moment nothing seemed to happen: the grand taxi continued to decelerate and the Russians' car edged ever closer behind them. Saif could see the furious glares of the men in the front seats. Svetlana thumped the dashboard with a frustrated shout.

And then the taxi jerked forward once more, as though pushed by an invisible hand, pulling away from the traffic behind. Slowly at first, almost intangibly; then, as Saif found his rhythm and pumped the crank around in endless clockwise revolutions, the car began to creep ahead of the traffic on either side, accelerating once more.

"Keep going!" Saif called down in reply

to Svetlana's excited shout. "Don't stop!" The words were as much for himself as for her, he realised. If he stopped winding the mechanism now, the taxi would only roll to a halt once more.

The Russians had clearly seen the results of his effort: their renewed attempts to push through the traffic met with shouts, curses and blaring horns, punctuated by the scrape and crunch of colliding metal. Now Saif saw a figure lever himself up from the passenger side of the Russians' car: bare headed, his tie whipping up against his face, he stretched out with one hand. Oh God, that makes sense – knock me off, and Svetlana can go no further...

Saif flinched to one side, turning the crank all the while. The bullet snapped against the taxi's bodywork, sparking unpleasantly.

He loosed one hand and grabbed at his belt for Foxwood's revolver. Now the only thing securing him to the back of the taxi was the crank itself. Deceleration or not, he would have to stop winding for a moment just to aim his shot.

He missed the Russian agent, but the bullet fractured the car's windscreen and it was forced to veer aside into the path of a heavier wagon. The man was crushed between the two vehicles with a scream that cut off abruptly.

Saif turned his attention back to the taxi's crank, renewing his efforts furiously. He was only dimly aware that they were past the outskirts of the city now, well on their way toward Menara. The traffic, however, was beginning to thin out – that made it less likely that Svetlana would collide with anything else, but at the same time it meant that the Russians would be able to close the gap more quickly. A glance back down the road told him that they had come to the same conclusion: the body of the dead agent hung limp from the passenger side, swaying as the Russian car cut across lanes of traffic in a bid to draw alongside them.

Saif managed to fire two more shots at the car, but he wasn't sure he had hit anything. Still, it was enough to force the Russians back a little further and buy Svetlana a bit more time. He thrust the revolver back into his belt, hoping that he had not used up the last of the ammunition – Foxwood had not passed him any spare rounds.

"Not far now!" he shouted.

"I see it," she replied. "Balloon!"

He translated that as the *Jane Grey*, and almost let the surge of relief that flooded through him slow his frantic work.

Another problem crept unwelcome into his mind: getting Svetlana through the rigid strictures of the departure lounge was going to be close to impossible. Foxwood had to have worked out some sort of arrangement with the officials, something either darkly surreptitious or high-handedly diplomatic – Saif could not imagine him doing anything other than at those extremes – but in the agent's absence there were bound to be delays and difficulties and the Russians would have no trouble at all in snatching Svetlana mere inches from safety.

The thought had obviously crossed her mind too.

"Hold on!" he heard her shout. The car swung off the pot-holed tarmac, crashing into the scrub at the side of the road, and Saif just had enough time to see the wire fencing ahead before jarring impacts flung him onto his stomach, gripping the winding handle with all of his strength.

The *grand* taxi bounced up off the uneven ground and hit the fencing at full tilt, Svetlana giving voice to a great whoop a fraction before the impact. Saif almost lost his grip, his legs flung outward and torn against the fractured mesh of the fencing. The weight of the revolver disappeared and he heard it clatter across the hood before flying off and away from view. His hands slipped further down the handle and he felt one leg brush the rear wheel of the car: he would be dragged underneath any second now, he realised.

"Stop!" he screamed, and prayed that she heard him.

The taxi skidded and fish-tailed, raising great clouds of dust from the dry, sandy soil. Saif let himself fall, and landed in a breathless heap, aching and bleeding, his muscles twitching with adrenalin and shock.

Svetlana stuck her head out of the window and regarded him dispassionately. "They still come," she told him. "Get back on."

He staggered back to the car and hauled himself onto the hood once more. The Russians had approached the fence more cautiously, he saw, but they were crossing the broken ground now. Saif forced himself to begin winding the crank once more, dredging up the very last of his strength.

Doors opened: the Russian car disgorged broad-shouldered agents and a pair of mechs, and they began to run across the scrubland, handguns drawn. Saif could only stare at them, uncomprehendingly, until another agent clambered onto the hood of the pursuing car and, as Svetlana hooted in triumph, realisation dawned.

Their mechanism had unwound.

"God is great!" Saif thumped the hood.

He turned the crank with renewed vigour and laughed as the Russian agents fell further and further behind. They fired their pistols at the taxi, but the distance had to be too great – one bullet smashed some of the rear lights, while the others ploughed into the ground and lifted slender wisps of dirt.

The *Jane Grey* loomed in the near distance: this ground belonged to the airport. The local police and security office, alerted by the sound of gunfire, had dispatched cars to intercept them. Saif judged that he and Svetlana would just beat them to the pad where the *Jane Grey* had been tethered. The Russians, even if they could reach the dirigible in time, would never be able to prevent her from boarding and escaping.

She slammed her foot down on the brakes mere inches from the edge of the pad, creating another cloud of swirling dirt. Saif abandoned the crank and limped across the tarmac with his hands raised high, peering through dirt and tears at the uniformed officers who had hurried down the airship's ramp.

"Who the devil do you think you are?" one exploded, his chin thrust out with incandescent rage. "You can't board His Majesty's ship dressed like *that*!"

Saif shook his head. "No, sir, not me, *her*. She is a personal guest of Mr Foxwood. She must board the *Jane Grey immediately*." He waved out to the Russians, struggling on foot over the scrub. "It is vitally important that she reaches England, sir."

Foxwood's name had checked the two officers, and now they shared a hooded glance. "Foxwood, eh?" the second man said, adjusting his hat. "You sure, boy? What's he like then? Can you describe him?"

Saif bit down a desire to shout and curse. "Hat. Beard. Quite short. Blows things up. Look, if you will not let her aboard then your government will not be pleased. Those are Russian agents over there, sir!"

Another shared look. Then the second man grunted. "Better take her up then, son. Get her out of sight. Clough, deal with these security fellas – tell 'em everything's on the level. King's business, and all of that. And tell 'em, if those are bloody Russians out there, I don't want 'em within a hundred damn yards of my ship. Got that?"

Clough eyed Saif with suspicion, but he nodded. "Aye captain."

The *Jane Grey*'s captain looked out at the approaching group of men and mechs. "Make that two hundred yards, Clough." He turned to Saif, who still stood exhausted at the foot of the ramp. "Come on lad: let's get the lady aboard. Then we'll break out the rifles. Give our paying customers a bit of excitement, what?"

"What?" Saif blinked.

The captain thumped him on the back and he stumbled forward. "Exactly. Now then, miss, I think you'd better take the other arm; catch him before he falls..."

His vision whirled and spun apart like overwound cogs.

His whole body vibrated gently. Wincing in pain, Saif levered himself up onto one elbow. The unfamiliar surroundings came into focus: panelled walls, including the one next to this bunk, which curved over his head; small port-holes that let daylight stream into the cabin; a porcelain hand-basin set in an ornate wooden frame, with a full jug of water next to it.

The *Jane Grey*, he realised.

Saif had taken passage by airship before, when he had studied in Spain, a voyage sponsored by Matif and the

Security Council. An extravagant method of travel, and he had found himself quite uncomfortable alongside the moneyed Europeans, but he looked back fondly upon the journey. Never once, however, had he believed he might one day wake up in an airship's first-class cabin.

He swung carefully around, his legs stiff and painful. The muscles in his arms and his upper back were also protesting heavily at the abuse they had suffered. His trousers had been roughly cut away so that his legs could be treated and bandaged, so now he looked as though he wore floppy shorts. He limped over to the washstand and splashed cold water onto his face, revelling in the clean, cooling sensation.

When he turned around, he was not

alone in the cabin.

"Well, you look worse than I feel, and that's saying something," the man in the steward's stiff white jacket said. For a moment Saif did not recognise him; then he realised that Foxwood, without his hat and sunglasses, somehow looked a completely different person.

"Sir! You made it!" He was stating the obvious, and knew he sounded stupid, but he couldn't think of anything else to say. "How...?"

Foxwood shook his head. "Long story, son, and we don't really have time to go into it. One day, perhaps, but for now let's just say that I told you I had a few more tricks up my sleeve." He motioned to the small side table just inside the door, where a tray with a teapot and two glasses now sat. "Take a pew for a minute."

The smell of freshly crushed mint leaves was refreshing. Saif slid awkwardly onto one of the chairs and began to pour.

"Where are we, sir?" he asked. A very slight swaying motion had given away the fact that the *Jane Grey* was no longer tethered to the ground at Menara.

"Just north of the Pyrenees," Foxwood said. "The weather looks fine all the way to Paris at the moment."

"And Svetlana – Miss Zakopalova?" he hurried to amend his question. "Is she safe now?"

"As safe as anyone can be at this height. Unless the bloody Russians managed to sneak somebody aboard before you even got to the airport, she's home free. Damn good job getting her there, by the way." Foxwood picked up his glass and picked out a mint leaf, flicking it onto a saucer with an irritated frown. "Too much of this stuff gives me the bloody runs, you know. Don't know how you can drink it all day."

The British agent stared up at the curving bulkhead for a moment and then returned his attention to Saif. "Matif – your uncle, isn't he? – he's not in a good way. The spywasps got him at least twice. Someone managed to get an antidote into him, but they're still not sure whether he'll pull through or not." He sighed. "He's a tough old bird though."

Saif bowed his head and said a silent prayer for his uncle, touched by the concern in Foxwood's voice. "What will happen now?"

Foxwood shrugged. "Lots of things. The Russians will complain, loudly, sulk, and kick a few toys from their dirty old prams. His Majesty will pretend he hasn't seen or heard a thing, and the Caliphate will do much the same. That bloody thing in space will bleep and parp its way around the Earth a few more times and then fall out of the sky. And, hopefully by the end of next year, the British Empire will put a man on the moon."

Saif gaped incredulously at the idea. "The *moon*? But how?"

"The same way they put that damned

Sputnik up there," Foxwood grinned. "A bloody great big rocket." Despite his avowed distaste, he poured another glass of tea. "Once we realised what they were up to over there, and just how far along they were, we told our idiot boffins to stop focusing so much on miniaturising everything and get us back in the race. Of course that's a bit of an over-simplification. But, anyway: there's a fair amount of science that we still haven't figured out. The Russians got there first."

"And Miss Zakopalova has all of that information?" Saif guessed, remembering what Matif had told him.

Foxwood nodded. "And now, more importantly," he said, "because she took great care to torch most of the research institute before she left, the Russians *don't*. They've put the Sputnik up there, but they've actually been put back by at least a year. With Miss Zakopalova in *our* hands, we have a brilliant opportunity to best the Russians at their own game."

Through the nearest porthole Saif could see a cityscape: the *Jane Grey* was descending in wide circles, yawing slightly. The ship's bell rang, three soft chimes to signal their imminent arrival.

"I hear they're already building the rocket," Foxwood said. He tapped the side of his nose to emphasise how hush-hush this information was. "All they need is what's in her head."

Emboldened by the other man's disclosures, Saif leaned forward over his tea. "Sir, that's the one part I understand the least. How is she carrying the information? She told me that she'd had an eye replaced at Alexandria, but I can't figure out the remainder."

Foxwood was silent for a moment. "This is strictly between us," he said, "although I imagine the Russians already have some idea of how she got the goods away."

He waited for Saif to nod his agreement before continuing. "Miss Zakopalova consented to the replacement of one eye with a prosthetic design, created by some of the best minds in your Caliphate. Of course we had a hand in it too: without the Vickers miniaturisation processes, how else could one make a functioning camera the size of a human eye?"

Saif could scarcely believe it. "A camera?"

Foxwood smiled. "A large capacity camera. With just one slight problem: the film was on a spool, and Miss Zakopalova cannot recall just how many shots she has taken. Hence the need for the cloth binding around her head – we cannot take the risk that the shutter mechanism takes more photographs on film that has already been exposed once. Do you understand that?"

Saif nodded. "Yes, sir." The response was almost automatic; he could not understand for the life of him how anybody could cope with such burdens and traumas.

"Right," Foxwood declared. "Back to your original question: *what happens now*? We have to leave you here, unfortunately. The Russians will be tracking the *Jane Grey* and, as unlikely as it may be that they're willing to crash a commercial airship, we just can't take that risk. You have this cabin as far as London, son. The registration is in your name now, with a Mrs al-Hamad also on the passenger list. Needless to say, she doesn't actually exist." The agent grinned. "Feel free to order a drink or two, son. It's on the Empire's tab, and I rather think you've earned it."

Saif looked around the small cabin for a moment. London – what on Earth would he do in London? "Sir, can I – I mean, would it be possible to see Miss

Zakopalova before you leave?"

"I thought you might ask," Foxwood said. "Quickly, then."

The bridge housed a wonderful array of brass instruments and pneumatics, levers, wheels and dials, all monitored by a team of pin-sharp officers. Every one of them, Saif noted grimly, wore a revolver upon his belt, the holsters unfastened for a quick draw. Two ratings stood either side of the hatch, with carbines cradled in their arms. The captain was clearly taking his security very seriously while Svetlana was aboard.

Svetlana was over on one side of the

bridge, where the captain had managed to set up a small table covered with a frilled cloth. It was currently laden with the devastated remnants of a full English tea. She stared out through the viewports at the city of Marseille, gently wheeling underneath the *Jane Grey*, and did not see Saif immediately when he and Foxwood entered – they were on her left side, Saif realised, where she had no sight.

The *Jane Grey*'s captain nodded to Foxwood and shot Saif a hard glare: a warning not to touch anything but the table, Saif thought, and even that only begrudgingly. "Excuse me, miss, you have visitors."

She had to turn to see them and so Saif stepped around to come into her line of vision. Svetlana's face immediately broke into a welcoming smile. She still looked more than exhausted, despite being refreshed with a bath and new clothes, but the tension of the pursuit had gone from her posture. "You wake! Sit, please."

Foxwood coughed discreetly. "We haven't much time, Miss Zakopalova."

She ignored him and indicated the other chair. Saif sat gratefully, his legs sore and complaining even after that short walk from the cabin. The bandage over her face, he decided, looked quite incongruous amidst the pomp of the airship's bridge.

After an awkward moment, in which each waited for the other to speak, Saif shook himself inwardly. "Mr Foxwood says that you are leaving here."

Svetlana nodded. "We take fast train to bridge of English Channel. Then, I do not know. But safe in England." She paused, then continued, taking care to find the words she needed. "I want to say thank you to you, for helping me to be alive. And to ask you – for I do not know your name?"

He blinked, then realised she must be right: she had allowed herself to be pushed, pulled and tugged away from the safe house by someone she had never met before, having to place blind trust in an absolute stranger. If he had ever doubted this woman's strength of will before, he would never do so again.

The smile came easily. "Saif. My name is Saif."

"Safe," Svetlana mispronounced. "Is true."

Foxwood coughed again, more impatiently this time. It would indeed be a swift farewell. Saif rose gingerly to his feet and then extended his hand to help Svetlana from the table. "I think you have to go," he said, and he hoped his voice did not betray the sadness he felt. "Maybe –"

Svetlana threw her arms around him, throwing him utterly off-guard, and he felt her cool cheek brush against his. "I do not forget, Saif," she whispered.

When she pulled away at last he thought there was a tear in her eye, but he could not tell for the emotion that had sprung his own. Her face was set in a thoughtful frown, as though she was trying to remember something. Then her mouth quirked and, before either Saif or Foxwood could react, she reached up to lift the bandage that covered the implanted camera-eye.

There was nothing that Saif could see that made the implant any different to her remaining, natural eye; it was a masterful work of art. And with her face fully exposed and lit, he realised again that he had been wrong. She *was* beautiful.

Her left eye glinted with the sharp movement of a shutter mechanism, and Foxwood cursed explosively. Then she lowered the bandage and tightened it once more. Wiping her hands, she turned to face Foxwood, the smile now set wide upon her face. "*That* one is for *me.*"

The agent exhaled in frustrated anger. "Good god, woman. Yes, all right. I suppose that's the very least we owe you. But, dear Christ, don't do that again!"

She shrugged. "Perhaps."

For the first time since Saif had met him, Foxwood looked to be at a loss. Finally he shook his head. "Look after yourself, son. And enjoy London. Captain, would you be so kind as to have your stewards fetch another tea for this young man? He looks half-starved."

With that, he ushered Svetlana quickly from the bridge. Saif eased himself back down at the table and watched the ground draw closer. If he could convince the captain to let him remain here, he might catch another glimpse of them as they left the airship.

Perhaps, he thought, wondering why it had not occurred to him before, somebody might even have a camera he could borrow.

About the Author

Steven Poore co-produced the Sheffield theatre premiere of Terry Pratchett's *Wyrd Sisters*. He is a founder member of the Sheffield SF&F Writers'.

His novel, *Heir To The North*, was shortlisted for Best Newcomer at the British Fantasy Awards in 2017.

He has featured in a number of anthologies with the BFS Award-winning publisher Fox Spirit Books.

Also by Steven Poore

Hair to the North

The High Kings Vengence

Art of War: Anthology for Charity

Legends 3: Stories in Honour of David
Gemmell

... and more.

We would like to thank everyone who
made this project possible,
via the Kickstarter and outside of it.

Specific thanks goes to:

Aaron Armitage

David Parker

Ross Warren

More dyslexic friendly

titles coming soon...